CHARLIE BROWN IS LOST!

Based on the Charles M. Schulz Characters

Designed by Terry Flanagan

Random House  New York

One day Snoopy took his scout patrol on an overnight hiking trip in the woods. After they had set up camp, the birds went into town to see the sights and have some fun.

When the birds returned to the camp, Snoopy noticed that Harriet wasn't with them.

It seemed that they had lost Harriet somewhere along the way.

But Harriet wasn't really lost. She was at the Humane Society.

Charlie Brown went to get her. Then he phoned his sister.

"Sally, I have Harriet with me. Now I have to try to find Snoopy. I just hope Harriet and I don't get lost in the woods."

"If you do, can I start moving my things into your room?" asked Sally.

"Don't worry, little bird," said Charlie Brown. "I'll help you get back with Snoopy and your friends."

Harriet chirped.

"It's no use talking," Charlie Brown said. "I can't understand a word you're saying!"

He looked around helplessly. "Well, bird, I hate to say it, but I don't have any idea where we are."

"Sally told me that Chuck isn't home yet. She thinks he must be lost in the woods," Peppermint Patty said to her friend Marcie. "Get your knapsack. Bring all the things you'll need in the woods. We're a rescue team!"

Marcie packed up.

"I have everything, sir," she said to Patty. "Food, water, and comic books."

"It may be a long trip," said Patty. "Better bring an extra comic book."

"This is embarrassing," Charlie Brown said. "I'm supposed to be leading this bird back to Snoopy, and now we're lost. . . . You know what I think, little bird? I think you should fly off and try to find Snoopy by yourself. Tell him I did my best! Tell him I'm lost! Tell him I'm sorry! Tell him 'Rats!' He'll understand!"

"Good grief, Marcie. How did you get so tall?" Patty asked her friend.

"It's my expedition boots, sir. While we're looking for Chuck, we might run into some bad weather. These boots are filled with goose down," said Marcie.

"Goose down?"

"Don't worry, sir," Marcie said. "If we meet a goose, you can pretend you don't know me!"

The two girls set off toward the woods.

Harriet soon found her way back to Snoopy and the scout patrol.

They were all happy to see her.

Harriet chirped excitedly and told everyone about her scouting techniques. But she forgot to mention Charlie Brown!

Snoopy decided that there had been enough excitement for one camping trip. He led the birds back home.

"Look, sir, it's starting to snow," Marcie said.

"My toes are cold," Patty said.

"You shouldn't have worn those sandals," Marcie said. "Maybe we can wrap your feet with comic books."

She tied some of the comics onto Peppermint Patty's feet with string.

The two girls set off again.

"If you walk slowly, sir, I can read your feet," Marcie said.

"Chuck, where are you?" Patty and Marcie shouted into the wind.

"We'll never find him this way, sir," Marcie said. "Maybe we should try something else."

"I think you're right, Marcie," Patty said. "How's this? Chuck, you dummy, where are you?"

Snoopy was resting on his doghouse when Sally came by.

"What are you doing at home?" she asked. "Your master's still out in the woods somewhere! What kind of dog are you?"

Snoopy sighed. He knew what he had to do.

The world-famous faithful dog braved the blizzard to go and look for his master.

"The comic books are coming loose from my feet, Marcie," Patty complained. "Pages are flying all over!"

"Let me see what I can do," Marcie said.

She kneeled down to fix the pages.

"Did you ever read this one, sir? It's where Spiderperson is on this bridge, and—"

"MARCIE!" shouted Peppermint Patty.

"Sorry, sir," apologized Marcie.

Snoopy forged ahead through the snow. He knew he had two choices. He could wander around looking and looking, or he could stand in one spot hoping that the lost person would come by.

He decided to stand still and wait for Charlie Brown.

Soon Snoopy was completely covered with snow. He knew he had made the wrong choice.

Snoopy began to walk again.

"Cats are lucky; they're never sent out to look for people," he thought. "Dogs always have to do the hard jobs. . . ."

Just then he passed Charlie Brown.

"Snoopy!" Charlie Brown cried happily. He pulled Snoopy over and gave him a big hug. "I bet you forgot who you were looking for!"

"Marcie, the comic books are coming apart again," Patty said.

"Look, sir!" cried Marcie. "I think I see somebody!"

It was Charlie Brown, coming toward them with Snoopy.

"CHUCK! How did you find us? We've been looking all over for you!" said Patty.

"We just followed the pages from some comic books," explained Charlie Brown.

"I see you made it home, big brother," Sally said to Charlie Brown that evening. "I thought you were lost for good, so I moved a few of my things into your room. The books and the record player will be easy to move back . . ."

". . . the dresser, the couch, the rug, the end
table, the lamp, and the bed will take a little
longer!"